MIKE MAIHACK

CLEOPATRA
IN SPACE

BOOK THREE
SECRET OF THE TIME TABLETS

graphix
AN IMPRINT OF
SCHOLASTIC

Copyright © 2016 by Mike Maihack

All rights reserved. Published by Graphix, an imprint of Scholastic Inc., *Publishers since 1920*. SCHOLASTIC, GRAPHIX, and associated logos are trademarks and/or registered trademarks of Scholastic Inc.

Library of Congress Control Number: 2015946169

ISBN 978-0-545-83868-9 (hardcover)
ISBN 978-0-545-83867-2 (paperback)

10 9 8 7 6 5 4 3 2 1   16 17 18 19 20

Printed in China   62
First edition, May 2016
Color flatting by Dan Conner and Kate Carleton
Edited by Cassandra Pelham
Book design by Phil Falco
Creative Director: David Saylor

CHAPTER ONE

6

AN ENTIRE XERX FLEET HAS US SURROUNDED.

KEEP THEM FROM ESCAPING.

DO NOT FIRE AT THEIR SHIP UNLESS YOU HEAR THE ORDER FROM ME.

HOW?

I DON'T KNOW.

BUT HE SOMEHOW LOCKED OUR CONTROLS SO WE AREN'T GOING ANYWHERE.

HERE, LET ME SEE.

BLOOP BLOOP BLOOP

BLOOP BLOOP BLOOP

BLOOP BLOOP BLOOP BLOOP

BLOOP BLOOP BLOOP BLOOP BLOOP

WE ARE SO DEAD, AREN'T WE?

HEY--WHERE'S ZAID?

BRIAN'S RIGHT.

WE'LL USE THE PODS.

THE PODS?

THE SHIP IS EQUIPPED WITH ESCAPE PODS--IN CASE OF AN EMERGENCY. THEY'RE SMALL, AND IF WE CAN DISTRACT THE XERX USING THE SHIP, THEY SHOULD DEPLOY UNDETECTED.

THAT'S A BIG **IF**.

IT'S OUR BEST CHANCE. CAN YOU GIVE US ONE LAST THRUST TO PUSH US AHEAD OF THE XERX?

IT'LL DRAIN THE LAST OF OUR FUEL.

WE WON'T NEED IT.

VWOOSH

OH.

WELL, WE CAN'T STAY OUT HERE. KHENSU SAID THE INFORMATION ABOUT THE TABLETS WAS **INSIDE THE CITY.**

YOU AND AKILA GO. I'M GOING TO STAY BEHIND AND SEE IF I CAN REPAIR THE LOCATION BEACON ON OUR POD. THERE'S A CHANCE KHENSU AND ZAID GOT OUT OF THE SHIP BEFORE IT EXPLODED.

I KNOW THEY DID.

THEY **DID.**

--AHEM--
YES, WELL, THEY'LL NEED TO KNOW HOW TO FIND US, SO PRIORITY ONE IS FIXING THE BEACON.

BESIDES, IT'LL BE MUCH EASIER FOR TWO TO SNEAK IN THAN THREE.

VERY CHIVALROUS OF YOU, BRIAN.

OKAY, SO WHAT'S THE PLAN?

ME?

YOU'RE THE LEADER.

DESTINED LEADER.

...

'ERE SEEMS AS GOOD A PLACE AS ANY.

ACTUALLY, I THINK I DO HAVE A PLAN...

VILE PLACE, TH' CITY. BETTER TA EAT OUT 'ERE IN TH' HOT SUNS WITH YOU THAN IN THAT FILTHY ENCLOSURE.

GOTTA MAKE A LIVIN' THOUGH, AH SUPPOSE.

SHOULD BE GRATEFUL THIEVES AND THUGS STILL MAINTAIN AN APPRECIATION FOR INTERIOR DECORATIN'.

'ERE'S TH' LAST BITE OF MAH SANDWICH. SORRY ABOUT IT BEIN' A BIT STALE.

OH, SURE. EAT AN' RUN.

EVEN TH' LIZARDS ON THIS PLANET ARE RUDE.

VVVVVVVVRRRRR

ɒʊLL∵ ⋂Ꝋꝺɾ.Ξ.

YEAH, YEAH. KEEP YER BLASTER HOLSTERED.

AH GOT MAH PAPERS RIGHT 'ERE.

FINNIAS FARSH. PEDDLER OF FINE CARPETS AN' TAPESTRIES.

WON'T FIND A FINER RUG IN ALL TH' NILE.

ꝭᏢᏢꝊ= ‖·ꞓꝺꝺ∵.

BEEP

ꝭᏒꝺᏢ∶ꝺ ꙄᏢ‖‖Ꝼ!

VVVUUMM

ENJOY HYKOSIS CITY?

CLACK

VVVVVVV

BLAZZT
BLAZZT
BLAZZT
BLAZZT

THIS PLACE LOOKS **GREAT!**

SHE'S TRYING TO KILL ME.

WHAT'S *HE* DRINKING?

OSIRIAN FIREWATER.

SOUNDS AMAZING.

YOU WANT YOUR CREDITS.

I GET IT.

SLACK YAH, AH WANT MAH CREDITS! THA'S WHY AH'M GRATEFUL FER THIS BOUNTY ON YER HEAD NOW.

WAIT--THE BOUNTY FROM OCTAVIAN?

YAH. WHAT OF IT?

HOW'S THAT ANY DIFFERENT FROM WHAT *I* DID?

YER JOB DIDN'T INVOLVE **ME** GETTIN' TA BEAT YOU TO A PULP.

ZAP!

IF THERE'S A BOUNTY ON THAT GUY, IT'S MINE.

YOU!

HI AGAIN.

WINK!

SHOT MAH HAT...

WHAT ARE YOU DOING?

WHERE'S THE SWORD?

WHAT?!

THEIR **HEADS.**

A HUNDRED CREDITS-- *EACH*--FER BOTH THEIR HEADS.

TRUCE?

TRUCE.

ZAP!

MY HAT!

WELL LOOK AT THAT...

NICE **GOLD** CROWN THERE, PRINCESS.

AH'M GOIN' TA ENJOY THIS EVEN MORE NOW.

BLAZZT!

CRASH

groan...

UM...SORRY ABOUT THE MESS.

'NUTHER ROUND, HANK?

OKAY, LET'S STAY OUT OF TAVERNS FOR, LIKE, THE REST OF OUR LIVES.

CLEO?

I WANT THAT SWORD.

irk.

I DON'T HAVE IT.

WHO DOES?

I GAVE IT TO OCTAVIAN.

OCTAVIAN?

THAT WAS PRETTY STUPID.

OUR PROFESSOR DID SOME ANALYSIS ON IT.

BEFORE *YOU* TOOK IT.

APPARENTLY THE SWORD WASN'T AS OLD AS IT SHOULD HAVE BEEN.

WHY WOULD...

grr.

AIN'T THAT THE ICING ON THE CAKE.

WHY ARE YOU TWO HERE ANYHOW? YOU DIDN'T TRAVEL ALL THE WAY TO THIS *NEON REFUSE HEAP* JUST FOR THAT SWORD, DID YOU?

UM... ONE SEC.

WHISPER WHISPER WHISPER

VRRRRRRZ

?

HE KNOWS ABOUT THE SWORD OF KEBECHET, HE MIGHT KNOW ABOUT THE TIME TABLETS AS WELL.

I DON'T TRUST HIM.

WELL, I DON'T TRUST HIM, EITHER, BUT WE NEED TO START SOMEWHERE.

CAN YOU THINK OF ANYONE ELSE IN THIS CITY WHO WOULD BE BETTER TO ASK?

HE DID KINDA HELP SAVE OUR LIVES BACK THERE.

BECAUSE OF A FIGHT *YOU* STARTED, I MIGHT ADD.

FINE.

THAT'S IT, THEN. C'MON, AKILA, LET'S--

SNAP !!!

BUT I MAY KNOW SOMEONE WHO HAS.

WHO?

AN ANTIQUARIAN. HERE IN HYKOSIS CITY.

DO YOU THINK THAT'S WHO KHENSU WAS PLANNING TO MEET WITH?

CAN YOU TAKE US TO HIM?

DEPENDS...

HEH HEH
SORRY!

BRUSH
BRUSH

BUT STILL--

NO **FUNNY**
BUSINESS.

YOUR FRIEND
ALWAYS THIS
INTENSE?

PRETTY
MUCH,
YEAH.

ALL RIGHT,
THEN. BETTER
GET GOING.

IT'LL TAKE AT
LEAST AN HOUR TO
REACH THE OTHER
SIDE OF THE CITY.

CHAPTER TWO

AN ORPHANAGE?

HELLO.

YOU LOOK JUST LIKE THAT PICTURE.

HUH.

HYKOSIS SEEMS LIKE A PRETTY LOUSY PLACE FOR AN ORPHANAGE.

ON THE CONTRARY, IT'S ONE OF THE BEST.

purrr

HYKOSIS'S LACK OF RESOURCES MAKES THE PLANET PRACTICALLY USELESS TO OCTAVIAN SO HE RARELY EVER BOTHERS WITH IT.

YES, THE FARTHER THESE KIDS ARE FROM THAT MONSTER, THE BETTER.

PLUS, THE PARENTING ABILITIES IN THIS CITY ARE **ATROCIOUS**.

HARKHEBI AND I ARE CONSTANTLY FINDING KIDS ON THE STREET IN NEED OF BETTER HOMES.

WHERE **IS** HARKHEBI?

IN HIS OFFICE. YOU TWO MUST GO BACK A WAYS. IT'S BEEN YEARS SINCE I'VE SEEN HIM PERK UP THAT MUCH AT THE MENTION OF SOMEONE'S NAME.

HERE. I'LL SHOW YOU IN.

YOU DON'T HAVE A **HOME**?

DON'T SOUND SO SURPRISED. I WAS SORTA STUCK IN A LIFE THAT DIDN'T REALLY SUIT ME.

TRUST ME. THIS IS BETTER.

LIVING ON THE STREETS WITH THE THREAT OF LOUD, UGLY BOUNTY HUNTERS CONSTANTLY AFTER YOU IS BETTER?

WELL, THE "LOUD UGLY BOUNTY HUNTERS" PART IS A RECENT DEVELOPMENT.

AND I'M NOT "LIVING ON THE STREETS." I HAVE MY SHIP. THE WHOLE GALAXY IS MY HOME NOW.

SOUNDS LONELY. I CAN'T WAIT TO SEE MY PARENTS AGAIN. HARD TO IMAGINE EVER RUNNING AWAY FROM THEM.

I DUNNO. I CAN UNDERSTAND NOT WANTING TO BE FORCED INTO A PARTICULAR LIFE. EXPLORING EVERYTHING ELSE THAT'S OUT THERE DOES SOUND ENTICING.

SEE, SHE GETS IT.

DON'T GET ME WRONG, I'D STILL MISS MY FAMILY.

HARKHEBI SORT OF IS MY FAMILY. HE TOOK ME IN WHEN I WAS YOUNGER. WE AREN'T AS CLOSE AS WE ONCE WERE BUT HE'S ALWAYS BEEN THERE FOR ME.

YOU'LL LIKE HIM. HE'S--

● ● ●

A XERX SOLDIER!

I THOUGHT THE XERX TENDED TO STAY AWAY FROM THIS PLANET.

THEY DO.

COULD BE A DESERTER BUT...

HMMM...

WE SHOULD FOLLOW HIM.

WHAT?

NO, SHE'S RIGHT.

I WANT TO SEE IF HE'S ALONE.

HUH.

WHERE'D HE GO?

OH NO.

THEY FOUND US. THEY FOUND ME.

WAIT--

YOU?

STUPID, SMELLY XERX!

LET GO OF ME!

POUND POUND

CRACK

SHOVE

ZAP!

YAY.
A WALL.

ANY IDEAS?

MAYBE WE CAN BLUDGEON HIS HEAD WITH SOME **FINESSE**.

UM... HEY...

WHAT?

YOU'RE...

ABOUT TO DIE?

YES.

THANK YOU.

NICE SHOOTING, RED!

A WHOLE **CREW** OF XERX?

YEAH, AND APPARENTLY WE NEED TO TELL JAVEL TO UPDATE THE SETTINGS FOR THE TARGET PRACTICE SIMULATOR.

I HAD MY GUN SET TO MAX AND IT **STILL** DIDN'T EVEN LEAVE A DENT IN THIS ONE.

CLAWG!

OW.

THAT...COULD BE ON ME.

I TOOK OUT A BUNCH OF THEM INFILTRATING OCTAVIAN'S SHIP BEFORE AGREEING TO STEAL HIS "PRECIOUS" SWORD OF KEBECHET. THAT WAS LIKELY THEIR CLUE TO UPGRADE THEMSELVES.

THE XERX CAN UPGRADE THEMSELVES?

WELL, YEAH.

THAT'S, LIKE, FIRST SEMESTER BIOLOGY, CLEO.

HUH. MAYBE I **SHOULD** START GOING TO CLASS.

DOES YOUR BIOLOGY CLASS EXPLAIN WHY SHE STARTED GLOWING?

YOU WERE **GLOWING**?

WHAT ARE YOU TALKING ABOUT?

BEFORE YOUR FRIEND SAVED OUR BUTTS. YOU... I DON'T KNOW...JUST STARTED GLOWING.

PINK.

I WAS GLOWING PINK.

UM, YEAH.

ARE YOU OKAY?

I'M NOT MAKING THIS--

HOLD ON.

"CLEO"?

YYYYES?

THAT'S SHORT FOR **CLEOPATRA**, ISN'T IT?

I **KNEW** I RECOGNIZED YOU THE OTHER DAY WHEN I, UH, **BUMPED** INTO YOU.

THE PROPHESIZED QUEEN OF THE NILE. **THAT'S** WHY THE XERX ARE HERE!

THEY COULDN'T CARE LESS ABOUT SOME PETTY THIEF LIKE ME.

THEY'RE AFTER **YOU**!

HEY--KEEP YOUR VOICE DOWN.

THIS ISN'T THE PLACE I WANT THAT TO BE COMMON KNOWLEDGE.

RECOGNIZED HER? HOW? YOU COULDN'T HAVE MET BEFORE THE WINTER DANCE, COULD YOU?

NO. OF COURSE NOT. THERE'S A DRAWING OF HER--WELL, SOMEONE SIMILAR TO HER--IN ONE OF HARKHEBI'S...

BOOKS.

WHAT'S WRONG?

IF OCTAVIAN IS AFTER YOU IT'S POSSIBLE HE'S AFTER WHAT YOU CAME HERE FOR, TOO, ISN'T IT?

WHAT IS THAT TABLET YOU SHOWED ME EARLIER?

IT'S CALLED THE ATA TABLET. IT MIGHT BE WHAT SENT CLEO TO THIS TIME.

WE AREN'T SURE OCTAVIAN EVEN KNOWS ABOUT IT, THOUGH.

ARE YOU KIDDING? OCTAVIAN KNOWS *EVERYTHING*.

HOW DO YOU THINK HE WAS ABLE TO CONQUER A QUARTER OF THE GALAXY?

AND IF YOUR FRIEND HARKHEBI HAS KNOWLEDGE OF ITS WHEREABOUTS...

WE NEED TO GET GOING.

NOW.

KHENSU!

IT'S BEEN TOO LONG.

YOU LOOK WELL, HARKHEBI.

YOUR **MOTHER** ISN'T HERE, IS SHE?

RELAX. I'M AWARE OF YOUR ISSUES WITH THE ADMINISTRANT.

I SEE YOU HAVE A NEW CARETAKER.

MOTHER?

ANNA MAE? YES, SHE'S BEEN A TREMENDOUS HELP. ESPECIALLY SINCE THESE OBSTINATE HIND LEGS OF MINE STOPPED LISTENING TO A THING I TELL THEM.

THANK GOODNESS FOR **TECHNOLOGY**, EH?

CLINK CLINK

I'LL GO BREW US SOME TEA.

SCOOT

VROOOO

OKAY. WHO **IS** THIS FOSSIL? AND HOW IS HE SUPPOSED TO HELP US FIND CLEO?

YOU SHOULD KNOW THIS OLD FOSSIL'S SENSITIVE CAT EARS STILL WORK JUST FINE. AND I WAS A GOOD FRIEND OF KHENSU'S FATHER WHEN I TAUGHT AT YASIRO ACADEMY.

KHENSU IS ACTUALLY A FORMER STUDENT OF MINE. WAS QUITE A GOOD ONE, TOO, DESPITE HIS MOTHER'S UPBRINGING.

IT'S BEEN YEARS SINCE WE LAST SAW EACH OTHER.

PROFESSOR OF HISTORY NOW?

nod.

IMPRESSIVE.

AND LOOK AT YOU, ZAID...

SSSS

ALL GROWN UP.

SHOULD...WE **KNOW** EACH OTHER?

WELL, I HAVEN'T SEEN YOU SINCE YOU WERE A SEEDLING.

YOUR FATHER AND MOTHER I KNEW QUITE WELL, HOWEVER.

VROOO

SCOOT

MY PARENTS?

MM-HMM. YOU MAY HAVE SEEN THE DRAWINGS OF THEM OUTSIDE. YOUR PARENTS MEANT A GREAT DEAL TO THIS ORPHANAGE.

VRROOOOOOO

leap

CIRCLE

SO THAT WAS...?

sit

I NEVER KNEW WHAT MY PARENTS LOOKED LIKE. I WAS TOLD EVERY IMAGE OF THEM WAS LOST.

MANY CHILDREN HAVE GROWN UP THAT WAY.

EVER SINCE THE BLIGHT.

I'M AFRAID OCTAVIAN'S DESTRUCTION OF OUR ELECTRONIC DATA HAD A FAR MORE DAMAGING EFFECT THAN HE EVER INTENDED.

WHAT...

WHAT CAN I TELL YOU OF THEM?

YOU MAY ALREADY KNOW YOUR FATHER, ZIYAD, WAS ORIGINALLY A SMUGGLER-- ILLEGALLY TRAFFICKING GOODS FOR PROFIT THROUGHOUT THE NILE.

OOEE OOEE

VKOOS

OOEE OOEE

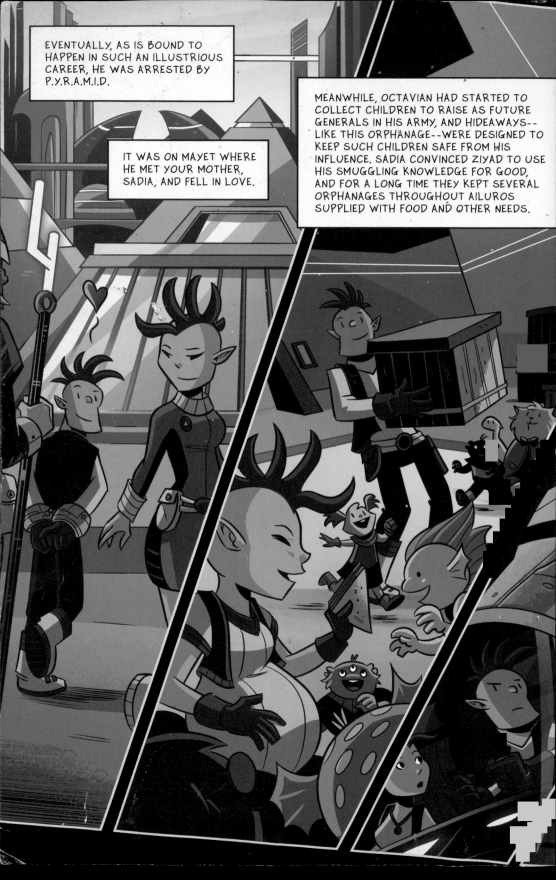

EVENTUALLY, AS IS BOUND TO HAPPEN IN SUCH AN ILLUSTRIOUS CAREER, HE WAS ARRESTED BY P.Y.R.A.M.I.D.

IT WAS ON MAYET WHERE HE MET YOUR MOTHER, SADIA, AND FELL IN LOVE.

MEANWHILE, OCTAVIAN HAD STARTED TO COLLECT CHILDREN TO RAISE AS FUTURE GENERALS IN HIS ARMY, AND HIDEAWAYS-- LIKE THIS ORPHANAGE--WERE DESIGNED TO KEEP SUCH CHILDREN SAFE FROM HIS INFLUENCE. SADIA CONVINCED ZIYAD TO USE HIS SMUGGLING KNOWLEDGE FOR GOOD, AND FOR A LONG TIME THEY KEPT SEVERAL ORPHANAGES THROUGHOUT AILUROS SUPPLIED WITH FOOD AND OTHER NEEDS.

VWEEEEEEEE

OH, THE TEA!

HEROES...

VROOO

MY UNCLE NEVER TOLD ME ANY OF THIS.

YES, HE ALWAYS DID SIDE MORE WITH YOUR FATHER'S CRIMINAL TENDENCIES. I'M NOT SURE HE EVER APPROVED OF HIS RELATIONSHIP WITH YOUR MOTHER, EITHER.

HOW IS YOUR UNCLE?

HE'S DEAD.

OH.

LOOK AT YOU, THOUGH. A **P.Y.R.A.M.I.D.** CADET!

IT'S WONDERFUL TO SEE ZIYAD'S SON GREW UP TO BE THE STRONG, RESPONSIBLE MAN I ALWAYS KNEW HE WOULD BE.

AHEM.

shake

NO?

WELL, HE'LL GET THERE.

MILK IN YOUR TEA, KHENSU?

OF COURSE.

rattle rattle

IS EVERYTHING ALL RIGHT, HARKHEBI?

I'M FINE. JUST THESE BONES OF MINE GROWING BRITTLE IS ALL.

NOW THEN, WHAT CAUSED YOU TO TRAVEL HALFWAY ACROSS THE AILUROS SYSTEM TO FIND ME, KHENSU?

GOOD QUESTION, GRANDPA.

BY NOW I'M SURE YOU KNOW YASIRO WAS RIGHT. CLEOPATRA ARRIVED EXACTLY WHERE AND WHEN HE SAID SHE WOULD.

I'VE HEARD WHISPERS. REASSURING TO KNOW THEY ARE INDEED TRUE. WHO KNEW THE OLD MAN WOULD TURN INTO SUCH A PROPHET?

THAT'S NOT ALL.

SHE KNOWS ABOUT THE **TIME TABLETS.**

BOTH OF THEM?

SHE KNOWS THERE'S A PAIR, BUT ONLY HAS ENOUGH INFORMATION TO LEAD HER TO THE ATA ONE FOR NOW.

YES, BUT THAT ONE WILL LEAD HER TO THE OTHER. THEY ARE CONNECTED, YOU KNOW. SHE AND THE TABLETS.

Sip

I'M AWARE, WHICH BRINGS ME TO WHY I'M HERE.

I THINK IT'S TIME THE TABLETS WERE REUNITED.

WHOA, WHOA. SLOW DOWN. WHAT THE SLAB IS A TIME TABLET?

THEY ARE THE ARTIFACTS RESPONSIBLE FOR YOUR FRIEND CLEOPATRA BEING IN THIS TIME PERIOD.

TWO TABLETS CALLED UTA AND ATA--BOTH CAPABLE OF IMMENSE POWER ONCE ACTIVATED BY THE CHOSEN ONE.

SO...THE PROPHECY **IS** REAL?

INDEED IT IS. AND REUNITING THE TABLETS WOULD ALLOW CLEOPATRA TO RETURN TO HER OWN TIME. AILUROS WOULD LOSE THEIR SAVIOR.

SHE'S JUST A TEENAGER, HARKHEBI--AND AN IMPETUOUS ONE AT THAT. WE ALL ENVISIONED HER **BLAZING** OUT OF THE SKY IN A CLOUD OF FIRE, SWORD OF KEBECHET IGNITED IN HER HAND, READY TO STRIKE DOWN OCTAVIAN AND HIS ARMY.

SHE'S YEARS OFF FROM BEING THE SAVIOR WE THOUGHT SHE'D BE.

YOU **WANT** TO SEND HER BACK.

I WANT THAT TO BE HER OWN DECISION.

Sigh.

I SUSPECT YOU'RE RIGHT. I NEVER THOUGHT IT WISE TO TRY TO CHART THE DIRECTION OF HER LIFE. ONLY TO PROTECT AILUROS.

YOU REALIZE I'LL BE BETRAYING YOUR FATHER'S TRUST IF I GIVE YOU THE ATA TABLET'S LOCATION?

YOU'LL ALSO BE PROVIDING **ME** WITH INTEL THE COUNCIL HAS BEEN TRYING TO GET AHOLD OF FOR YEARS.

HAHA!

TRUE.

VROOOO SCOOT

SPIN

STOP

BLOOP

I PACKED YOU SOME SANDWICHES.

UM... THANKS.

IT'S ABOUT A HALF-DAY WALK TO THE TOMB. I ASKED ANNA MAE TO GIVE YOU SOME PROVISIONS.

tug tug

YOU SHOULD HAVE THIS.

THANK YOU, HARKHEBI.

YOU'RE DOING GREAT WORK HERE.

IT IS REFRESHING TO BE SURROUNDED BY SUCH **YOUTHFUL** SPIRIT.

PERHAPS ONE DAY I'LL MEET OUR YOUTHFUL MESSIAH.

STAY SAFE.

AND ZAID, REMEMBER THERE IS MORE TO HEROISM THAN WHAT'S WRITTEN IN SCROLLS.

I'LL BE IN MY OFFICE FOR A WHILE, ANNA.

PLEASE, NO DISTURBANCES.

VROOO

SHUFF

THERE.

FOLLOW THEM, AND YOU'LL FIND WHAT YOU WANT.

IT'S AMAZING. AFTER ALL THE INFORMATION I'VE OBTAINED IN THIS GALAXY...

THAT THERE ARE PLACES THAT PEOPLE STILL BELIEVE ARE HIDDEN FROM ME.

IN HIS OFFICE.

WHAT'S WRONG?

STAY QUIET! IT'S NAP TIME.

NAP TIME?

HARKHEBI?

HARKHEBI?

KNOCK KNOCK

HOW LONG HAS HE BEEN IN THERE?

NOT LONG.

VSCHH

HE ASKED NOT TO BE DISTURBED.

COOL.

HARKHEBI!

WHERE'S OCTAVIAN, HARKHEBI?

WHAT HAPPENED?

PEN.

COUGH

PARCHMENT.

I'VE GOT IT.

YOU THOUGHT A PEN AND PARCHMENT WERE VITAL SUPPLIES TO BRING TO HYKOSIS?

HOW MANY *TEXTBOOKS* HAVE YOU ALSO BEEN LUGGING AROUND IN THAT BAG?

JUST TWO.

COUGH COUGH

HERE YOU ARE.

SCRITCH SCRITCH

COUGH COUGH

NOT MUCH TIME.

OCTAVIAN LIKELY ALREADY HAS THE TABLET.

THE TABLET?

THIS IS WHERE THE **ATA TABLET** IS?

CLEOPATRA.

SO GLAD I GOT TO SEE--

COUGH COUGH COUGH

HE WON'T BE ABLE TO...

CONTROL...

THE GOLDEN LION IS...

AARRGH!

ZWIP ZWIP ZWIP

VWUMP
VWUMP
VWUMP

WHAT DID HE WRITE?

UM...A MAP, I THINK?

ALSO A BUNCH OF NUMBERS.

I'LL BE HONEST. I HAVE NO IDEA WHAT I'M LOOKING AT HERE.

LET ME SEE IT.

IT'S A FLIGHT PATH.

I CAN TAKE US THERE.

US?

SHOULDN'T YOU STAY HERE AND...Y'KNOW, HELP?

ANNA IS MORE THAN CAPABLE OF TAKING CARE OF THINGS. IF YOU'RE GOING AFTER OCTAVIAN, I WANT IN.

BESIDES, IF YOU WANT TO GET THERE UNDETECTED, YOU'LL NEED **MY** STEALTH SHIP.

ALL RIGHT THEN...

LET'S GO KICK SOME OCTAVIAN BUTT.

124

CHAPTER THREE

WHAT ARE YOU DOING?

I'M GOING TO SHOOT HIM.

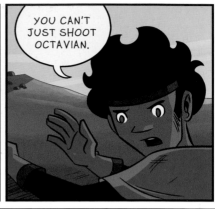

YOU CAN'T JUST SHOOT OCTAVIAN.

WHY NOT?

HE'S *OCTAVIAN!*

I'M NOT GOING TO KILL HIM, JUST **STUN** HIM SO, I DUNNO, P.Y.R.A.M.I.D. CAN CAPTURE HIM OR SOMETHING.

THAT'S NOT WHAT I--**ACK**, NEVER MIND.

GO AHEAD. YOUR FUNERAL.

ANTONY'S RIGHT, CLEO. YOUR GUN BARELY SCRATCHED THAT XERX SOLDIER EARLIER.

WE NEED A BETTER PLAN THAN JUST RUNNING IN THERE ZAPPING AWAY.

WELL, WE GOTTA DO **SOMETHING**, AKILA!

THEY HAVE KHENSU AND ZAID!

HOW HANDY DO YOU THINK YOU STILL ARE WITH A SLINGSHOT?

POK

YOU SHOULD HAVE THOUGHT TWICE BEFORE INFILTRATING **MY** SHIP.

DETAIN HIM.

ᐃᑉᑉᕁ.

VRUM

NOW, IF YOU ARE DONE PLAYING AROUND, I BELIEVE THERE'S A TABLET YOU WERE LOOKING FOR.

THE ATA TABLET IS IN THE TOMB, CLEO. HE USED ZAID AND ME TO GET INSIDE BUT THE TABLET WON'T ACTIVATE WITHOUT YOU.

HE **WANTED** YOU TO FIND IT.

MY CARELESSNESS BROUGHT YOU RIGHT TO HIM.

DON'T BE RIDICULOUS, KHENSU. I WOULD HAVE FOUND A WAY TO HYKOSIS WITH OR WITHOUT YOU.

DOESN'T MEAN I'M GOING TO HELP THIS TENTACLED FREAK.

THEN YOUR FRIENDS DIE.

IT'S OKAY. DO AS HE SAYS.

I'LL BE WITH AKILA.

grr.

FINE. AFTER YOU.

NO, I INSIST...

PROFESSIONAL SLINGSHOT ARTISTS FIRST.

IS THAT **ALL** IT SAYS?

UM...

IT'S ON THE TABLET. GO ON. YOU STARTED READING IT LONG AGO, MIGHT AS WELL FINISH IT.

DEATH'S DAUGHTER BETRAYED BY A KISS. RA'S KINGDOM EXCHANGED WITH A HISS.

FIRE WILL SWALLOW WATER, FEAR WILL CONQUER BLISS.

IN THE STARS, A HERO WILL COLLAPSE THE ABYSS.

nod

WITH SWORD OF KEBECHET IN HAND, THE QUEEN OF THE NILE WILL MAKE HER STAND.

A FINAL BREATH, A LAST COMMAND,

SHE'LL LIGHT THE DARKNESS THAT THREATENS THE LAND.

"A FINAL BREATH..."

WHAT DOES THAT MEAN?

KHENSU?

IT MEANS YOU'RE DESTINED TO DIE.

AKILA!

oOOoh...

ARE YOU ALL RIGHT?

MY...MY ARM.

I CAN'T...

WE WERE ATTACKED. OCTAVIAN HAS CLEO.

I HAVE A PLAN, THOUGH.

CAN YOU SNAP THIS OFF THE BOTTOM OF MY BOOT?

GRAVITY PROPULSORS!

QUICK-- WEDGE THE PROPULSOR UNDER YOUR BOULDER. ITS MAX SETTING SHOULD PROPEL IT OFF YOUR ARM.

Snap.

GDĿ≠Ż!

CALM DOWN, **SULFUR BREATH.** WE WERE JUST CHATTING.

FOOM

MOVE!

ZWIP

I WAS WONDERING WHEN YOU'D RECOGNIZE ME.

WHAT...WHAT **HAPPENED** TO YOU?

HOW ARE YOU...?

HOW'D YOU GET ALL...

WORMY?

THIS. THE CURSE OF THE **TRUE** SWORD OF KEBECHET HAS KEPT ME ALIVE, IF NOT IN THE MOST PRISTINE CONDITION.

I'VE WAITED A VERY LONG TIME TO FIND YOU. IN THIS TIME. IN THIS PLACE. TO FINALLY HAVE A WAY TO CORRECT THE UNIVERSE.

BUT IF YOU ARE UNWILLING TO COMPLY, I SUPPOSE I WILL HAVE TO TAKE MATTERS INTO MY OWN HANDS.

168

YOU'RE **AWAKE!**

WELCOME BACK TO THE LAND OF THE LIVING, SLEEPY-HEAD.

WHAT...?

OOOOoo

CAREFUL. YOU'VE BEEN OUT FOR ALMOST THREE WEEKS.

THREE WEEKS!

HOW-- HOW DID I...

YOU DEFEATED *OCTAVIAN*, CLEO!

WELL, SORTA.

P.Y.R.A.M.I.D. SCOUTS REPORTED SPOTTING HIM AND HIS FLEET NEAR MENDESIA.

HE SEEMS TO HAVE LEFT THE AILUROS SYSTEM ALONE, THOUGH. FOR NOW, AT LEAST.

BRIAN MANAGED TO GET THE LOCATION BEACON ON OUR ESCAPE POD REPAIRED. P.Y.R.A.M.I.D. FOUND HIM, NOTICED ALL THOSE STUNNED XERX OUTSIDE THE TOMB, AND BROUGHT US BACK HERE. WELL, EXCEPT ANTONY. HE DISAPPEARED PRETTY MUCH AS SOON AS P.Y.R.A.M.I.D. ARRIVED.

YEAH, WHO *IS* THIS ANTONY GUY? NOT SURE I LIKE HIM.

AND ALL HIS JUMPING. AND "CUTENESS."

SHUSH, BRIAN. ANTONY'S COOL.

HOW ARE YOU FEELING?

LIKE A CAVE COLLAPSED ON MY HEAD.

WHAT ABOUT ZAID?

OH.

YEAH.

YOUR ARM...

ISN'T IT **GREAT**? BRIAN CREATED IT FOR ME.

IT'S STILL A PROTOTYPE. ALL I COULD MUSTER IN THREE WEEKS.

I'LL MAKE A BETTER ONE.

V RR

AKILA...

SO I GUESS I MISSED ALL THE ACTION, BUT IT SOUNDS LIKE YOU AND THE TABLETS ARE CONNECTED, AFTER ALL. LIKE MAGNETS.

AKILA TOLD ME YOU DISAPPEARED FOR A FEW SECONDS. DO YOU KNOW WHERE YOU WENT?

CLEO-- *WAIT!*

AAH!

CAN SOMEONE PLEASE FIND ME SOME PANTS?

≥Snicker≤

CLACK

WHIRRRRRRRRRRR

THUNK

fwoosh

LIKE MAGNETS...

YASIRO HAD THE SCHOOL BUILT AROUND IT.

HE PREDICTED YOUR ARRIVAL WOULD BE LINKED TO THE UTA TABLET'S LOCATION. THAT'S HOW KHENSU KNEW TO BE IN THIS ROOM WHEN YOU APPEARED.

I FIGURED IT WAS ONLY A MATTER OF TIME BEFORE ITS PRESENCE PULLED YOU BACK HERE.

HE LIED TO ME. YOU **ALL** LIED TO ME. YOU HAD A WAY TO SEND ME BACK TO MY OWN TIME ALL ALONG.

NO, **YOU** HAD A WAY. WHEN I SAID THE POWER THAT SENT YOU HERE WAS NOT FROM US, THAT WAS THE TRUTH. THE TABLETS SEEM TO ACTIVATE BY YOUR TOUCH ALONE.

YOU REALLY ARE THE CHOSEN SAVIOR.

YOU PUT THAT BOOK ABOUT THE TABLETS IN THE LIBRARY, DIDN'T YOU? YOU **WANTED** ME TO FIND THE ATA ONE.

SO KHENSU...

DID AS I EXPECTED. HE BROUGHT THE ATA TABLET TO US. ALL HE NEEDED WAS A LITTLE PUSH TO SEND HIM AFTER IT.

YOU AND YOUR FRIENDS PROVIDED THAT PUSH.

WHERE **IS** KHENSU?

ON SUSPENSION UNTIL FURTHER NOTICE. DESPITE RETRIEVING THE ATA TABLET, WE STILL LOST A CADET ON HYKOSIS. PLUS, KHENSU INTENTIONALLY WITHHELD KNOWLEDGE OF THE TABLET'S WHEREABOUTS FROM THE COUNCIL.

THE COUNCIL. HOW DO **THEY** FEEL ABOUT ALL THIS?

NOW THAT BOTH TABLETS ARE IN OUR POSSESSION, WE'RE DISCUSSING WHETHER WE SHOULD INDEED ALLOW YOU TO USE THEM TO GO BACK TO YOUR OWN TIME.

IS THAT WHAT YOU WANT?

GOZI--

OCTAVIAN--

IS STILL OUT THERE--WITH THAT STUPID SWORD--AND I CAN'T HELP BUT FEEL... THE WAY HE IS...

HIS ACTIONS...

ARE ALL SOMEHOW MY FAULT.

I WILL DISCUSS YOUR FEELINGS WITH THE COUNCIL.

BLOOP

WRRRRRRR--CHACK

FOR NOW, I THINK IT'S BEST YOU GET SOME REST.

PHARAOH YOSIRA!

BOW

I'M GLAD YOU'RE OKAY.

SHE'S ALL YOURS.

CLEO!

WERE... WERE YOU JUST TALKING TO *PHARAOH YOSIRA*?

UM...YEAH. SORT OF.

WOW.

WHAT IS GOING ON? WHY'D YOU RUN OUT OF THE MED WARD SO QUICKLY?

OH, IT'S... NOTHING.

I WAS JUST WORRIED ABOUT KHENSU.

I HAVEN'T SEEN HIM SINCE WE GOT BACK.

I THINK HE'S IN TROUBLE FOR EVERYTHING THAT HAPPENED ON HYKOSIS.

YEAH.

C'MON. LET'S GO HIT THE TARGET PRACTICE RANGE.

ARE YOU KIDDING?

YOU JUST WOKE UP FROM A **COMA**.

COMA SCHMOMA. I WANT TO SEE IF AKILA'S ANY BETTER WITH HER FANCY NEW ARM.

OH, JUST WAIT TILL YOU SEE THE ENHANCEMENTS BRIAN INCLUDED!

VRR

YOU MIGHT NOT BE THE BEST SHOT IN THIS SCHOOL ANYMORE, CLEO.

Pff.

WE'LL SEE ABOUT THAT.

ARE YOU OKAY, CLEO?

A LOT HAPPENED ON HYKOSIS.

YEAH, I'M FINE. **GREAT**, ACTUALLY.

IT'S JUST...

SPECIAL THANKS TO:

My incredibly supportive (and patient) family: Jen and Oliver and Orion Maihack, Sam and Barb Maihack, Brian and Jill Maeda, Patrick and Kim Tally, John and Darci Roberts, Chad and Jen Roberts, KeAli'i and Lindsey Rozet, Randy and Janice Meade, and everyone else I wish I had room to include here (there are so many of you now!).

My chill office companion, Misty. Your purring eased the stressful bits of this book. My attention-craving office companion, Ash. I still miss you.

The superheroic folks at Scholastic (including but not limited to): Cassandra Pelham, David Saylor, Phil Falco, Lizette Serrano, Sheila Marie Everett, Tracy van Straaten, Bess Braswell, Denise Anderson, and Ed Masessa.

My agent, Judy Hansen. Please don't ever leave me.

Christ, for the various paths You presented to me this year, giving me the freedom to choose which ones to take, and then preparing me for what I found along the way.

Google Images, for your endless array of cowboy hats.

EXTRA SPECIAL THANKS TO:

All of the teachers, librarians, booksellers, parents, and readers out there who have supported Cleopatra in Space thus far. YOU GUYS ARE AWESOME!

ABOUT THE AUTHOR

A graduate of the Columbus College of Art & Design, Mike Maihack spends his time, well, working on the Cleopatra in Space series. He is the creator of the popular webcomic *Cow & Buffalo* and has contributed to books like Sensation Comics Featuring Wonder Woman; *Parable*; *Jim Henson's The Storyteller*; Cow Boy; *Geeks, Girls, and Secret Identities*; and *Comic Book Tattoo*. *Cleopatra in Space: Secret of the Time Tablets* is Mike's third graphic novel, following *Target Practice*, which won a Florida Book Award, and *The Thief and the Sword*. He lives with his wife, two sons, and Siamese cat down in the humid depths of Lutz, Florida.

Visit Mike online at www.mikemaihack.com and follow him on Twitter at @mikemaihack.